BEARNARD
WRITES A BOOK

To Christopher T. Leland —D. U.

To all book lovers trudging, flying, or
dancing through Storybook Land —M. S.

Henry Holt and Company, *Publishers since 1866*
Henry Holt® is a registered trademark of Macmillan Publishing Group, LLC
120 Broadway, New York, NY 10271
mackids.com

Library of Congress Control Number: 2021917024

Our books may be purchased in bulk for promotional, educational, or business use. Please
contact your local bookseller or the Macmillan Corporate and Premium Sales Department
at (800) 221-7945 ext. 5442 or by email at MacmillanSpecialMarkets@macmillan.com.

First edition, 2022
The art for this book was created using Adobe Photoshop.
Printed in China by RR Donnelley Asia Printing Solutions Ltd.,
Dongguan City, Guangdong Province

1 3 5 7 9 10 8 6 4 2

ISBN 978-1-250-26145-8

BEARNARD
WRITES A BOOK

Written by **Deborah Underwood**
Illustrated by **Misa Saburi**

GODWINBOOKS

Henry Holt and Company
New York

Bearnard and Gertie were reading about the brave bear in *Bearnard's Book*.

"I wish you had your own book too, Gertie," said Bearnard. "I know! I will write a book about you!"

"My own book? How exciting!"
Gertie said.

Bearnard got some paper.
He got a pencil.
He sat at his desk **and thought.**

And thought.

And thought.

Gertie waited patiently. "Is the book ready yet?" she called.
"Not quite yet," said Bearnard.

"Gertie?" said Bearnard. "I do not know *how* to write a book."

"I know you can do it. Maybe you just need some help," Gertie said.

"Of course!" Bearnard said. "I'll ask the Queen of Storybook Land!"

Bearnard and Gertie walked to Storybook Gate.

"May we please see the queen?" Bearnard asked.

"I'm sorry, Bearnard," said the sentry. "She's not here right now. May I help you?"

"I want to write a book about my good friend Gertie," said Bearnard. "But I've lost my way."

"Ah!" said the sentry. "Then you need this!"
He handed Bearnard a map.
"First stop: the library!" Bearnard said.
"I love libraries!" said Gertie.

Gertie browsed while Bearnard read and read.

"I am inspired!"
Bearnard said. "What's next?"

"Character City!" said Gertie.
"Let's go!"

"Wow!" said Gertie. "Look at all these characters!"
"We already have one character for your book: you!"
said Bearnard. "Who else should I choose?"

"How about a dragon?" Gertie asked.
"Too dangerous," Bearnard said. "How
about a bunny?"
"How about a crocodile?" Gertie asked.

CHOOSE YOUR CHARACTERS!

"Maybe that cute little worm," Bearnard said.

"Bearnard!" Gertie said. "I want to be in an exciting story! A story that's full of adventure!"

"Definitely the worm," said Bearnard. "What's next?"

"Setting Village. Let's go!" said Gertie.

"Where would you like your story to take place?" asked Bearnard.

"A volcano!" said Gertie. "That would be exciting!"

"How about a lovely park?"

"A crumbling iceberg!" said Gertie.

"Oh! That pond looks safe," Bearnard said.

"Your story will take place in a pond. You know how to swim, don't you, Gertie?"

"I am a goose!" said Gertie. "Of course I know how to swim!"

"Right," said Bearnard. "What's next?"

"Problem Plaza!" Gertie said. "Now *that* sounds exciting!"

"Gertie!" Bearnard cried. "You're my friend! I do not want you to have *any* problems!"

"Bearnard," Gertie said. "It is only a story. Maybe I am being chased by pirates!"

"Let's find a *teensy* problem. Maybe you lost your sock,"
said Bearnard. "Or broke your crayon."

"Maybe I need to battle a rampaging monster!" said Gertie.

"Broken crayon it is," said Bearnard.

Gertie sighed. "All right, Bearnard. What's next?"

"The Writers' Room!" said Bearnard.

Gertie relaxed with her book while Bearnard wrote.

WRITE YOUR STORY! THEN REWRITE IT TO MAKE IT EVEN BETTER!

Pencils   Paper   Mugs   Tea & Coffee

Once upon a time, there was a wonderful goose named Gertie.
She lived in a pond with her worm friend Edgar.
One day Gertie broke a crayon.
So Gertie and Edgar went to the store and bought a new crayon.

The End.

Bearnard stared at the story.
It wasn't very exciting.
And Gertie wanted an exciting story.

"How's it coming?" Gertie asked.
"I am going to take a thinking walk," said Bearnard.

Bearnard walked all over Storybook Land.
"Can a writer add characters to a story?"
Bearnard asked the sentry.
"Of course!" said the sentry. "Writers change
things all the time! That's part of writing."

Bearnard began to get ideas. Exciting ideas. After all, it *was* only a story. And he did want to make Gertie happy. Bearnard ran back to the Writers' Room and wrote . . .

and wrote . . .

and wrote.

"Gertie!" he finally shouted.
"I am done with your story!"

"Thank you, Bearnard!" Gertie said. "And it is fine if it is not full of adventure. I am just happy to have my own story."

Bearnard cleared his throat and read:

Once upon ~~a time, there was a wonderful~~ goose named (Gertie.) ~~She lived in a pond with her~~ worm friend (Edgar.)

~~One day Gertie broke~~ her ~~a~~ crayon. ~~So Gertie and Edgar went to the~~ ~~and bought.~~ To buy

Once upon a time, Gertie and her friend Edgar the worm were drawing beside the pond.

Gertie broke her crayon, so they decided to buy a new one.

But just then a pirate ship appeared!
"Give us your loot!" said the pirate king.
"We only have a broken crayon!" Gertie said.
"Then we will feed you to our crocodile!" the
pirate king said.

Gertie and Edgar tried running.
But the pirates were too fast.
Gertie and Edgar tried hiding.
But the pirates found them.

Then Gertie remembered that
pirates like peanut butter.
She tossed a jar down the hill.
The pirates scrambled to get it.

Then Edgar turned into a dragon.
"Wow, Edgar! You're a dragon!" said Gertie.
"Surprise!" said Edgar.

"Can you fly us to a volcano?"
"Sure!" said Edgar.

They flew to an iceberg.
While they waited for the crayon to cool off,
Gertie battled a rampaging monster.

After the monster surrendered, Gertie
checked the crayon.
"It's ready!" said Gertie. "Let's fly home and
get back to drawing."

And they did.

The End.

"What do you think?" Bearnard asked nervously.

"Bearnard!" said Gertie. "That was the best story ever! Thank you!"

She gave him a big hug.

"Our books look so nice together on your shelf!"
Gertie said.

"You could write a story too," Bearnard said.
"We have the story map to help us!"

"No, thank you," Gertie said. "In the library, I discovered something wonderful. My great-great-great-great-grandgoose was a poet! I am going to write poems, just like she did."